14.95

TAP-TAP

by Karen Lynn Williams
illustrated by Catherine Stock

CLARION BOOKS • NEW YORK

Clarion Books
a Houghton Mifflin Company imprint
215 Park Avenue South, New York, NY 10003
Text copyright © 1994 by Karen Lynn Williams
Illustrations copyright © 1994 by Catherine Stock

Illustrations executed in watercolor.
Text is 16.5/23 pt. Weiss.

Printed in the U.S.A.

Library of Congress Cataloging-in-Publication Data

Williams, Karen Lynn.
  Tap-tap / by Karen Lynn Williams ; illustrated by Catherine Stock.
    p.   cm.
  Summary: After selling oranges in the market, a Haitian mother and
daughter have enough money to ride the tap-tap, a truck that picks
up passengers and lets them off when they bang on the side of the
vehicle.
  ISBN 0-395-65617-6
  [1. Haiti—Fiction.   2. Trucks—Fiction.   3. Markets—Fiction.
4. Mothers and daughters—Fiction.]   I. Stock, Catherine, ill.
II. Title.
PZ7.W66655Tap   1994
[E]—dc20   93-13006
                                                     CIP
                                                      AC

HOR 10 9 8 7 6 5 4 3 2 1

For Susannah,
whose experience inspired this story
—K.L.W.

For the Williams family,
who opened their home to me
and their hearts to the people of Haiti
—C.S.

It was early on market day when Sasifi and her mama started down the path to the main road. The sky was still gray. Mama carried a big basket of oranges on her head. Sasifi carried a smaller one.

"Will we ride in the tap-tap today?" Sasifi asked.

"No," said Mama. "We will walk to market, the same as always."

The sky turned rose and then blue. Sasifi's basket grew heavy. She had been to market with Mama before, but today was the first time she carried her own basket. Now that Sasifi was eight, Mama said she was big enough to help on market day.

Finally they reached the big road. Many people were walking. Some rode on slow tired horses. Others led donkeys with heavy loads of sugarcane and bananas. Sasifi wished she could ride a donkey or a horse, or better still, speed along in a tap-tap.

"Look, Mama." Sasifi stopped and watched a brightly painted tap-tap rumble toward them.

"Come, Sasifi," Mama called, "or we will be too late to sell our oranges."

A woman on the side of the road waved, and the tap-tap stopped. The woman lifted up her baskets. A man helped her climb on.

"If we take a tap-tap," Sasifi said, "we will get there in plenty of time." Already the new sun was hot. Sasifi's feet were tired. Her neck ached.

"We don't have money for the tap-tap," Mama said. "Perhaps you are not yet big enough to help me on market day."

Sasifi stretched her body taller and took big steps to keep up with Mama. Of course she was big enough to help!

As they reached the marketplace, crowds of people were
gathering: women with baskets and men with lumber, pigs,
and goats. *Bep-bep!* A big red and yellow and blue tap-tap
pulled up and a lot of people got off. Sasifi wished she were
one of them.

Inside the market Sasifi saw women selling brooms and men selling little chairs. A man had a stack of straw hats for sale. "Look at the pretty hats," Sasifi called to Mama, but Mama didn't stop. Sasifi had to push her way through the crowd to catch up. Everywhere, the market women chattered noisily like Madam Sarah birds in their nests.

Mama found a space among the other fruit and vegetable ladies and Sasifi helped count their oranges out in piles of five. She dusted each one with a handkerchief to make it clean and shiny. Mama showed her how to match the bigger oranges with the smaller ones so the piles would be even.

All morning Sasifi watched Mama calling to the shoppers and making change. When the sun was overhead, Sasifi curled up on their mat and slept.

9

10

Later, Mama went to do her marketing. She left Sasifi behind to sell the rest of the oranges.

"If you sell any oranges, be careful making change," Mama warned. "And tie your money tightly in your handkerchief." She disappeared into the jostling, noisy crowd.

"Here," Sasifi called to the shoppers as she had seen Mama do. "See my beautiful oranges. They are bigger and sweeter than the others. I can give you a good price."

Mama was surprised when she returned. "Have you eaten all my oranges?" she asked Sasifi.

"No, Mama, I have sold them all." Proudly Sasifi unwrapped the handkerchief she had tied around her waist and gave Mama the coins.

Mama counted the money and smiled. "You have done a good job," she told Sasifi. "I have a surprise for you." She reached into her market basket and pulled out a pretty woven hat with a wide brim and a red band. "This will keep the sun out of your eyes on our journey home."

"Mama, it's beautiful," Sasifi exclaimed. "Thank you. Thank you!" Sasifi had never had a fine new hat before. She placed it on her head, tilting it this way and that until it felt just right.

"Now," Mama said, handing Sasifi some coins, "buy yourself a treat before we go. Quickly."

Sasifi could hardly believe her good luck. It was the first time she had had money of her own to spend at the market, and she knew just what she would do.

"Come, Mama," Sasifi said. She passed the market stalls
where men were selling fresh bread. She passed the ladies
selling sweet peanut candy and bonbons in bright paper
wrappers. When she got to the man selling juice in plastic
bottles, she stopped for a moment and looked at the bright
colors—red, green, orange, purple. She knew the juice was
sweet and icy cold, and for a moment she couldn't decide.

"Hurry," Mama said behind her. "We must go."

Sasifi squeezed the coins tightly in her hand and made up her mind. "Yes," Sasifi told Mama, "and we will ride the tap-tap."

"Ah!" Mama said. "A tap-tap. I should have known. We will both get to rest our tired feet. Thank you, *chérie*."

Sasifi ran ahead of her mother to the place where the tap-taps stopped. One big tap-tap piled high with people and baskets and huge bags of charcoal began to pull away. "Wait," Sasifi called, but the tap-tap did not stop.

"Here!" A man waved to Sasifi and her mother. "I have a place for you." The man's tap-tap was freshly painted with green and blue and orange designs on the side, and in front there were beautiful flowers and birds. Across the top, Sasifi read the word HOPE.

"Do you go to Deschapelles?" she asked the driver.

"Yes, *chérie*."

"Come, Mama," Sasifi called. She climbed into the truck and chose the last seat so she could see out the back. The man helped Mama with the baskets. She sat on the bench next to Sasifi.

"We are ready," Sasifi called to the man. "We can go."

"Not so fast, *chérie*," the man said.

"Just two people cannot pay for the ride," Mama explained. "We must wait for others."

Soon a man came with four small new chairs. The driver helped him tie the chairs on top of the tap-tap. The man climbed in the back. A woman came with a crying goat. The goat did not want to get on the tap-tap. The driver had to pick it up, holding its legs so it wouldn't kick.

"Will we go now?" Sasifi asked.

"Not yet," Mama told her.

Another woman came with a basket on her head and a chicken under each arm. Mama took her chickens as she climbed on board. Next came a man with a huge round basket full of bread. He passed the basket into the truck. The smell of fresh bread reminded Sasifi that she was hungry.

The hat man came with dozens of hats piled on his head. He smiled at Sasifi. Sasifi reached up and touched her beautiful hat. She wiggled with excitement. Surely we will go now, she thought.

The driver banged the side of his truck two times. "This car for Deschapelles," he called to the people leaving the market. A tired woman came with a baby in her arms and a little boy clinging to her dress. They all climbed in. Mama

squeezed closer to Sasifi. Sasifi was squashed against the end of the tap-tap. A hard chain pressed into her side. She tried not to think about the cold juice and sweet bonbons she had left behind in the market.

"The tap-tap is full," she told Mama. "Won't we leave soon?"

"Soon," Mama said.

A man came carrying a table on his head, and on the table were piled bowls and jars of good things to eat. The people in the tap-tap passed the table back. The man climbed on. A boy with a bundle of sugarcane climbed on. He tossed the sugarcane on top of the tap-tap. There were no seats left, so he stood up in front of Sasifi.

The driver banged the side of the truck. "Good," he said. "We will go."

"Wait, wait, *monsieur,* wait." One more woman was coming toward the tap-tap. She was a very big woman. She could not run fast and she was huffing and puffing. The woman carried two big baskets of yellow bananas, two big pineapples, and a watermelon.

There is no place for her, Sasifi thought, just as the man next to Mama squeezed her closer to Sasifi and the boy across from her took the two big pineapples. Someone pushed the big woman up on the tap-tap.

Finally Sasifi felt the truck begin to move. Bump, bump. Sasifi held on to her hat as their tap-tap began to go faster and faster. Bump, bump, squeak. They sped past mud huts with green and pink doors and shutters, and pretty houses with gingerbread trim. They passed tired donkeys with heavy loads and little children who stopped to watch and wave. Sasifi waved back, proud to be riding in a tap-tap.

Tap-tap! The man with the hats banged on the side of the
truck. The truck stopped and the man got off. Everyone
spread out a bit and the tap-tap started up again.

Sasifi liked the feel of the wind in her face. She held on
tight to her beautiful new hat and laughed at the goats
jumping over one another at the side of the road.

Tap-tap! The woman with the chickens hit the side of
the truck. The tap-tap stopped and the woman climbed
down. She took her chickens and the tap-tap began to move
again.

Two boys began chasing after them. Faster and faster went the tap-tap. Faster and faster went the boys. They tried to jump on the back. "No, no," cried the man next to Mama. Finally the boys gave up and stopped, panting, in the middle of the road. Everyone in the tap-tap laughed.

Tap-tap! The man with the chairs hit the side of the tap-tap and it stopped again. The man climbed down and everyone spread out. He took his chairs off the top of the tap-tap and they took off again.

Bep-bep! The tap-tap horn blew loudly. Chickens scattered and a big old pig squealed. The tap-tap sped past green rice fields and leafy banana trees. Sasifi held on tight with both hands.

Suddenly she felt her hat lift right off her head. In a
swoosh it was gone.

Sasifi saw her beautiful new hat fly off behind the tap-
tap. "My hat! Stop! My new hat!" she called, but her voice
was lost in the wind.

"Stop," she cried again as her beautiful hat with the red band rolled in the dust behind them. The tap-tap did not stop.

"Mama," she cried. Mama was talking to the lady with the baby. She didn't pay attention to Sasifi. Sasifi's hat was a speck on the road.

"Help," she called. The tap-tap squeaked and rattled. The driver couldn't hear.

Sasifi tugged on Mama's arm. Then she knew what to do.

Tap-tap! Sasifi banged as hard as she could on the side of their pretty painted truck.

She felt the tap-tap slow down and stop. "My hat!" she called. She pointed, and several small children at the side of the road raced to save her hat.

"*Merci,*" she called to them when her hat was safely on her head and the tap-tap started again.

Bep-bep! The driver waved as they passed another tap-tap coming toward them. Sasifi squeezed her eyes shut to keep out the dust, but she didn't let go of her new hat.

Tap-tap! This time it was Mama asking the driver to stop. Sasifi and Mama climbed down and took their baskets. Sasifi straightened her new hat and gave the driver her coins.

The colorful tap-tap began to shake and rattle down the road. "*Au revoir,*" Sasifi called, waving her hat.

Sasifi danced ahead of Mama down the path to their village. Mama laughed. "So, you are not too tired after a busy market day?" she asked.

"Oh, no, Mama." Sasifi held on to her new hat and twirled around. "Not after riding on the tap-tap!"